DANGER!

The dam reared above them as high as a house at its highest point, grayish white and curving from shore to shore.

Danny pointed to a spot some distance above his head. In the concrete, there was a crack about two feet long and wide enough to admit the blade of a knife. Brown water was oozing slowly out of it and trickling down the face.

"Oh!" Irene exclaimed suddenly. "Look!"

Before their eyes, the crack had seemed to jump. It was longer, a couple of inches longer, and wider. Not much, but enough so that a real stream of water, as thick as a pencil, came bubbling out.

"Let's get out of here," Danny cried. "We've got to tell somebody!"

Danny Dunn and the Universal Glue

Jay Williams and
Raymond Abrashkin

Illustrated by Paul Sagsoorian

AN ARCHWAY PAPERBACK
POCKET BOOKS · NEW YORK

**POCKET BOOKS, a Simon & Schuster division of
GULF & WESTERN CORPORATION
1230 Avenue of the Americas, New York, N.Y. 10020**

Copyright © 1977 by Jay Williams and Raymond Abrashkin

Published by arrangement with McGraw-Hill, Inc.
Library of Congress Catalog Card Number: 77-78764

ISBN: 0-671-41495-X

First Pocket Books printing March, 1979

10 9 8 7 6 5 4 3 2

AN ARCHWAY PAPERBACK and ARCH are trademarks
of Simon & Schuster.

Printed in the U.S.A.

This book is for Guy and Danielle Sawers, friends of Danny's and of mine.

J.W.

Contents

Danny
Dunn
and the
Universal
Glue

1
The Lemonade River

It promised to be a perfect day for fishing. The air was full of the scent of bush honeysuckle and bee balm. There were just enough fleecy clouds to keep the sun from being too hot. And drivers waiting for the lights to change at the corner of U.S. Route 2, which led out of Midston, looked wistfully at the three young fishermen on their bikes who crossed the highway on their way to the hills.

There was something unusual about those three. Two of them, a tall, thin, sad-looking boy, and a pretty girl whose brown hair was tied back in a careless ponytail, carried rods and lines. But the third, a freckled, redheaded boy, had a large cardboard box fastened behind his bicycle saddle.

Someone else thought it was strange. A boy on a dashing ten-speed racer drew up alongside them.

"Hey!" he called. "Whatcha going to do, Danny—get the fish to jump into that box?"

Danny Dunn grinned, but said nothing.

The sad-looking boy, Joe Pearson, looked over his shoulder at the newcomer. "Dynamite," he said.

"Huh?" said the boy on the ten-speed racer.

"Oh, Joe, why do you even bother talking to Eddie?" said the girl. "He's just a pest."

"I'm not talking to him," Joe answered. "I'm talking to his bike. It's a nice bike and I don't want it to get hurt."

"Wise guy," said Eddie, steering closer to Danny. "What do you mean, dynamite? It's against the law to dynamite fish."

"Who said anything about dynamiting fish?" said Joe. "We're going to blow up the dam. Then, when all the water runs out, we'll just walk around on the bottom picking up all the fish we want."

Eddie Phillips scowled. "Oh, yeah? Well, if it's dynamite, let's see if it'll explode," he snarled.

He let his bike coast, and lifting a foot,

kicked at Danny in the hope of knocking him over.

But Danny wasn't there. The instant Eddie took his foot off the pedal he had guessed what was coming. Swiftly he swerved to one side. Eddie's foot lashed thin air and he lost his balance. He went sprawling one way and his bike, its wheels spinning madly, the other. Luckily, he landed in the grass at the side of the road.

Danny had almost gone over himself, but he managed to straighten his wheel and slowed down, as did his friends. Irene Miller looked back at Eddie.

"Oh, gosh," she said, "do you think he's hurt?"

Eddie answered her by sitting up and rubbing his arm. "I'll get even with you, Danny Dunn!" he howled.

"There's nothing wrong with his voice," said Joe. "Are you okay, Dan?"

Danny was making sure his box was still tied on firmly. "Sure," he said. "Let's go. He won't bother us anymore."

They rode on in silence for a moment or two, and then Joe said, "Listen. You've been very mysterious ever since we started. Come on, Dan, tell us—what *is* in that box?"

"I told you, it's a new invention of mine,"

Danny said. "You'll find out when we get there. All I'll say is that it's going to be the biggest thing since the invention of the fish hook."

"I'll bet I can guess one thing about it," Joe grumbled, bending over his handlebars. "If it's like any of your other inventions, it'll mean trouble."

"Oh, Joe, don't be such a pessimist," Irene laughed.

"Yeah? Well, what about that wind-driven pencil sharpener he made? When he hooked it up outside the classroom window, the windmill broke loose and almost took the principal's head off."

"Even Einstein made mistakes," Danny said loftily.

Danny Dunn had been familiar with science almost from the time he could walk. When he was a baby, his father had died and his mother had gone to work for the noted scientist, Euclid Bullfinch. Danny had teethed on a slide rule, and his first toy had been a digital computer. His friend, Irene Miller, who lived next door, was as keenly interested in science as he was. She was the daughter of a professor of astronomy at Midston University, and her biggest problem was deciding whether she wanted to be a physicist or a biologist when she grew up. The third member of the trio provided a good balance, for Joe Pearson failed all his math courses with dreary regularity, and knew nothing about molecular theory, but was the pride of the whole school for the plays, poems, and stories he wrote.

They turned their bikes off the hardtop road into the old logging trail that ran through the woods. It was hard going, for the dirt surface was rutted and pebbly. After half a mile, they left their bikes beside a big rock and set out on foot. It was cooler under the trees. Soon they emerged on the bank of a quiet little stream which slipped gently along between boulders and the overhanging branches of witch hazels and willows. The rounded tops of the low, wooded Midston Hills rose all about like the edges of a bowl, and it was so quiet that it was hard to believe they were only a couple of miles from a busy town.

They walked along the bank for a short distance until they found a deep pool where the stream curved around some rocks. Irene and Joe turned to watch Danny, who began to untie the string around his box.

"Go ahead," he said. "It'll take me a minute or two to get ready."

Irene opened her bait can and quickly

baited her hook with a fat worm. She looked up to see Joe watching her with a peculiar expression.

"What's wrong?" she said.

"Listen," he said, and cleared his throat. "I—I—listen, Irene. Will you bait my hook for me? I can't stand to hear the worms scream."

Dan had taken out a contraption of wire and netting, jointed rods, pulleys, and cord. Carefully, he fitted it together. Joe studied it with his head on one side.

"Wow! It's some kind of monster," he said. "Will it bite?"

"Go ahead and laugh," Danny replied. "It's my special anglerfish snap-trap."

It looked, in fact, something like a butterfly net except that the open end was hinged so that it opened and closed like a pair of gaping jaws. One rod held the upper part; a second, with an arrangement of pulleys and a line, closed the bottom. Small sinkers weighted the net, and inside it a piece of wire held a baited hook.

Danny said proudly, "It's modeled after a fish I once saw in a museum. It was called an anglerfish, and it had an enormous mouth full of teeth and a little flippy sort of thing dangling in front of it like a line with bait on it. When any small fish nibbled at it, *snap!* it got eaten."

Irene was inspecting his invention. "I see," she said. "This is something like that, only you have the bait inside the net, sort of inside its stomach."

"That's right. And all I have to do is wait for a fish to swim into the mouth of the net. Then I pull this cord to close the jaws, and I've got him."

"Pretty smart," Irene said with admiration. "I wonder if it'll work."

"We'll soon find out," said Danny.

He stepped out onto a rock above the pool and lowered his apparatus into the water. He had a little difficulty, at first, because he had to hold the two rods one above the other so that the jaws of the net would open and close properly. However, at last he got himself settled. Joe went a bit farther down and dropped his hook into the stream, while Irene found another, smaller pool where she was sure she had spotted a trout under an overhanging ledge.

They angled in silence for a while. Joe was more interested in Danny's invention than in his own fishing. He kept glancing over to where the anglerfish snap-trap could be seen dangling in the clear brown water.

At last he said, "You ought to have another line to hold the pointed end of the net up. It's sagging."

"I'd need three hands," Danny answered. He tried to look down, but it was hard to do while keeping his balance on the rock and holding both rods.

Then Joe whispered, "There's a fish sniffing the mouth of the trap."

"Fish don't sniff," Danny replied, also in a whisper.

"This one is. Now he's moving away. No, he's coming back."

Danny craned his neck. "I can't see him."

"He's a big one. He's looking it over."

"Where is he?"

Danny leaned forward, trying to see around his own arms. A little farther, a little farther still, and suddenly—

"Wups!"

Splash!

Dan came to the surface spluttering and gasping. The pool was small enough so that two or three strokes took him to the side. Joe and Irene dropped their rods and ran to catch his outstretched hand, although they were laughing so hard they weren't much help. He floundered ashore and shook himself like a puppy.

"You always were a great one for diving into things headfirst," wheezed Joe.

"Oh, me," said Irene, still giggling. "I'm sorry I laughed, Dan, but you did look so surprised."

Danny didn't answer. He was staring into space with a perplexed frown.

"What's the matter?" Irene said, sobering.

Joe went up to Danny and waved a hand in front of his eyes. Dan paid no attention.

"He must have hit his head on a rock," Joe said in alarm. "He's got concussion.

Brain damage—a fractured skull! He's unconscious!"

"Oh, quit it, Joe," Danny said, grinning and pushing his friend away. "It's nothing like that. It's the water."

"What do you mean, the water?" said Irene.

Danny knelt beside the stream, scooped up some in his palm, and tasted it.

"Yep! I thought so," he said. "It's got a funny taste. In fact, it tastes—it tastes like—"

"Poison?" said Joe.

"No," Danny answered. "Lemonade."

2
The Sandwich Accident

"I was right—it's brain damage," said Joe. "He's raving."

Irene, however, stooped to the water and tasted it as Dan had done. She rose with a grimace.

"I see what you mean," she said. "Not exactly lemonade, but it is kind of sourish. Or maybe tangy."

"You're both driving me crazy," Joe said. "Wait a minute, let the old master taster try it."

He filled his palm and sipped. He smacked his lips and looked thoughtfully at the sky. "They just forgot to put any sugar in it," he said. "And they made the lemonade with sea water. Otherwise, it isn't bad."

"You'll eat or drink anything," said Irene. "You're a kind of human garbage pail. I wonder what it is, Dan. Could it be something dissolving into the stream from the rocks?"

Danny shook his head. "I doubt it. We fished this stream last summer and I don't remember anything wrong with the water. Do you? I bet you something is running into it from farther upstream."

"Pollution? But there isn't any factory or farm along it. Nothing but woods. Of course, we've never been right to the end of it."

Danny scratched his head and then seemed to realize for the first time that he was dripping wet. "Lucky it's a hot day," he said. "Lend me your rod, Irene. I want to fish out the snap-trap."

She handed it over, and as he dropped the hook into the pool and tried to snare the meshes of the net, she went on. "What do you think we ought to do? If something is polluting the stream—"

Joe clutched at his throat. "And I drank it!" he cried. "Help, help!"

"Relax," Irene said. "That little sip won't kill you."

"No, but it may ruin my taste buds."

"I know one thing I'm going to do," Danny

said. He had caught the net and was pulling it up. "I'm going to tell my mother about it."

Joe reached over and grabbed the dangling net. He carefully unhooked it and put it on the shore. "Do you think she can get them to put some sugar in it?" he said.

"She's the head of the Citizens' Environmental Committee," said Danny. "If there's something wrong, they'll want to know about it."

"That's a good idea," Irene agreed. "Are you going to go now? Maybe you'd better—then you can put on some dry clothes."

Danny looked hungrily at the stream, at his net, at the fishing rods. He said slowly, "There's no point in my rushing home. Mom's out today, at some kind of meeting. And by the time I got home, I'd be dry anyway. And I haven't really had a chance to try the snap-trap. And—"

"That's enough," said Joe, picking up his rod. "You've convinced me."

It was nearly noon when Danny parked his bicycle in his own driveway. He carried the cardboard box into the kitchen. He hadn't caught anything in the snap-trap, but he had been able to study its action and to figure out some shortcomings—the jaws didn't close fast enough, for one thing, so that inquisitive fish had a chance to escape. His mind was buzzing with ideas for improvements, but when he got into the house he remembered the strange taste of the brook.

He put his box in the hall, and called, "Mom!" There was no answer. He went back to the kitchen and made himself an everything sandwich—leftover tuna salad, a slice of cold chicken, a piece of cheese, a slice of tomato, a leaf of lettuce, plenty of mayonnaise, and some peanut butter—and with this in one hand and a paper napkin in the other to catch the drips, went to see if Professor Bullfinch was in his laboratory.

The Professor's inventions had brought him in enough money so that he could afford his own private lab. It was built on the back of the house, a large, light room crammed full of equipment, and a smaller office in which the Professor kept his files, notebooks, and reference books. It had a door connecting it to the rest of the house, and another leading out to the garden so that the Professor could step outside and walk about, thinking and smoking his pipe.

When Dan looked in, Professor Bullfinch was perched on a stool at one of the stone-topped lab benches, intently studying a complicated arrangement of test tubes, tall glass jars, and glass pipes through which an amber-colored liquid circulated. A couple of Bunsen burners hummed and popped, and there was a hot smell in the air that stung the nostrils. The Professor's round, usually jolly face was set in concentration. He wore a rubber apron, but in spite of it his baggy tweed trousers were spotted with fresh stains.

"Hi, Professor," Dan said, through a mouthful of sandwich. "Do you know where Mom is?"

"That's good," said the Professor.

"I have to tell her something. It may be important."

"Did he?" said the Professor, making a note on a pad beside him.

"Did who what?" Danny said in puzzlement, coming nearer.

Professor Bullfinch raised his head and peered at Dan through his thick-rimmed glasses. "You aren't making much sense, my boy," he said. "Aren't you feeling well?"

Danny sighed. Usually the Professor was far from absent-minded, but when he was thinking hard about a problem he was apt to be vague.

"I'm sorry," Dan said. "I shouldn't have interrupted you. I'm all right. I was just asking you if you'd seen my mother."

17

"Dear me, I'm afraid I wasn't really listening. My fault." He fixed his gaze on Dan's sandwich. "What a handsome and unusual construction. An experiment, I presume? It looks as though you've tried to see how many different things you could combine before the whole operation exploded."

Danny held out the sandwich. "Have a bite? There's plenty."

"No, no, I really couldn't. Well, I am rather hungry," said the Professor as Dan persisted. "I seem to have lost track of the time." He took a large bite and handed the sandwich back.

"What are you working on?" Danny asked.

"Bullamuh," answered the Professor. He swallowed his mouthful. "Polymers," he said. "You know what they are."

"Chains of giant molecules formed by lots of smaller ones sticking together," Dan said promptly.

"Quite right. I've got a rather interesting new organic polymer here which is displaying some rather odd characteristics. I don't suppose you could spare another bite of that giant molecule—I mean sandwich?"

"Sure." Danny handed it over and settled himself companionably on another stool.

Professor Bullfinch munched dreamily. "I

don't believe there's ever been any real research done into the extraordinary pleasures of sandwiches," he said. "Now, there's a project! Why is it that when you put almost anything between two slices of bread, it tastes better? Is it the enzymes released by the bread? Some sort of molecular interaction? Or a purely psychological response to the pleasures of picnics and outdoor—"

He was cut short by a loud blopping sound from behind him. The liquid in the tubes had become thicker and was producing slow, heavy bubbles.

"Good heavens!" cried the Professor. "I forgot it."

He spun round and reached out to turn off the Bunsen burners. Unfortunately, the hand he thrust out was the hand holding the remains of the sandwich. The filling had become rather slippery, what with mayonnaise, the juicy tomato, and the damp lettuce leaf. At his violent movement, everything went flying. The lab bench was showered with a shrapnel of chicken, tuna, cheese, and all the rest of it.

That wouldn't have been so bad, except that both Danny and the Professor involuntarily tried to catch the stuff in midair.

Their hands met at the web of glass tubes and pipes, and slowly, grandly, the whole

thing toppled over and fell to the floor with a crash.

After a moment, the Professor sighed. "Ah, well," he said, "there's nothing quite so exciting as the smash of so much glass."

"Oh, gosh!" Danny quavered. "Was that my fault?"

"To be fair, I think it was mostly mine." The Professor put down the two pieces of bread, which were all that was left of the sandwich. "Never mind. I have all my notes, and there's plenty more glassware on the shelves."

Danny circled the bench to look at the pool of liquid among which splinters glittered.

"Well," he said, "I'll clean up the mess. It won't take a minute."

There was a concrete sink in one corner, and he filled a bucket from its faucet and got a mop. He dashed the water over the puddle of amber stuff. He put the pail down and lifted the mop. He blinked, looked again, and slowly lowered the mop.

"Professor," he said, "take a look at this."

Professor Bullfinch took his glasses off, wiped them, and put them on again. He squatted down to see better.

Wherever the water had touched the amber liquid, it had hardened into a shining film like a sheet of very thin glass.

"Stiff water!" said Danny in astonishment.

He reached out to touch it, but the Professor caught his wrist.

"Not so fast, my boy," he said. "Don't be rash."

He found a long glass stirring rod on the lab bench. With this, he touched the surface of the water. His face took on a puzzled expression.

"What's the matter?" asked Danny.

Slowly, the Professor let go of the rod. It remained upright, stuck fast to the liquid on the floor.

"Bless my soul!" he said.

He pulled out his pipe and began deliberately filling it.

Danny stared at the long glass rod, which looked as if it were growing out of the floor like the stalk of some odd kind of plant.

"How did it do that?" he said. "Is it some sort of glue?"

Professor Bullfinch struck a match and held it to the bowl of his pipe. Between puffs, he said, "I am going to—have to—think about this."

His round face shone in the curling smoke like a beaming moon among clouds. Returning to the stool, he sat down and picked up his notebook.

"Professor Bullfinch," Danny said softly.

The Professor nodded. "Some sort of glue?" he murmured, almost to himself. "Perhaps so. But if so, a wonderful sort."

Danny waited a moment, but the Professor said no more. After a few moments, Dan tiptoed out of the lab. It would have made no difference if he had clumped. The Professor was deep in thought, and little short of an earthquake would have roused him.

3
Universal
Glue

Mrs. Dunn was in a snappish mood. Her meeting had lasted much longer than expected, and before it was over she had a headache. She was hot and sticky. She had planned a lovely tomato-and-tuna salad for dinner, but when she made her mayonnaise in the blender something went wrong and it turned into a kind of oily soup. She had had to throw it away and send Danny out to buy commercial mayonnaise, which she didn't like nearly as much. She dropped one of her best platters and broke it. Professor Bullfinch had had to be called three times for dinner, and to cap all, when he came wandering in with his hands behind his back, he said innocently, "Did you call me?"

Mrs. Dunn gave him a fiery glance.

"Euclid Bullfinch," she said, "I have had a very trying day. Unless you want me to blow up in a cloud of screams, you had better sit down at once and start eating."

The Professor hurriedly took his seat. "My dear Mrs. Dunn," he said, "I'm very sorry. I have been working on something extremely interesting—something I owe to an invention of Danny's."

"An invention of Danny's?" Mrs. Dunn repeated. She lost some of her annoyance and began dishing out the salad. "What was it?"

"A sandwich," said the Professor.

Mrs. Dunn began to laugh in spite of herself. "You'd better explain."

"Danny built a most attractive sandwich and let me have some of it. I was working on an experiment at the time, and forgot to stop the operation. As a result, the material was subjected to too much heat, and that accident produced a surprising result."

Danny had been listening quietly. He put in, "What did you find out? Was I right? Is it a kind of glue?"

Professor Bullfinch nodded. "It is certainly an adhesive. And one with astonishing powers. It will hold just about anything to anything else. It will stick together stone, metal, plastic, wood, cloth, glass. It can be made to do so slowly or instantly. It will hold two separate pieces of something as firmly as if they were one piece. It will even—if you can imagine such a thing—stick two pieces of water together!"

"Is that what I saw?" said Danny.

"Yes, in a way. In fact," the Professor finished, "you might call it a universal glue."

Danny forgot the food on his fork. "How does it work?" he asked.

"Spoken like a true scientist," smiled the Professor. "That's what I've been investigating: how and why. What you saw happen to the water that touched the stuff gave me the clue, of course."

"Danny," said Mrs. Dunn. "You've always been able to do two or three things at once. You can listen and eat at the same time."

"Sure, Mom. Go on, Professor."

"Well, to begin with, there's the larger picture: Why do things hold together in the first place? Why doesn't this tabletop just fly apart into a million atoms? There is a kind of bond between the molecules that make up matter. That bond is presumably electromagnetic.

"Water is particularly good at making a close intermolecular contact with other materials. And in fact, nearly everything in the world has a monolayer of water strongly adsorbed to it—that is, clinging to it by electrostatic action. Water, you know, is H_2O, two atoms of hydrogen and one of oxygen. The double-negative charge of the oxygen atom and the positive charges of the hydrogen atoms set up a magnetic attraction which holds each molecule of water to most surfaces."

"What's a monolayer?" asked Mrs. Dunn, who was so interested that she had forgotten to eat her own dinner.

"A layer just one molecule thick. All clear so far?"

"I think so."

"Well, my new polymer has an affinity for water. That means it attaches itself to the layer of water molecules on a surface very strongly. And since almost everything in the world has that monolayer of water bonded very strongly to *it*, the polymer will stick to everything. In short, this new substance is quite different from any other glue you've ever heard of—it depends for its action on a universal electrostatic force, and so it really *is* a universal glue."

"If that's the case," said Danny slowly,

"you could stick bricks together and build a building with it."

"I'm sure you could."

"It sounds marvelous," said Mrs. Dunn. "Maybe you could use it to stick the pieces of my best platter together. I dropped it this afternoon."

"I'm not quite ready for practical applications yet," said Professor Bullfinch with a chuckle. "I still have some problems to solve in handling the stuff, as you can imagine. Ask me again in a day or two."

When dinner was over, Professor Bullfinch settled down in the living room with his bull fiddle, which he played, as he said, to help him think while relaxing. As the deep tones of the music filled the house, Dan and his mother companionably cleared away the dinner things. Danny had just finished drying plates, when Irene knocked at the screen door.

"Hi," she said. "I came over to find out what your mother said."

"Huh? She didn't say anything."

"Nothing at all?"

"Well, she said hello, and then she told the Professor to sit down and eat—"

Irene raised an eyebrow. "I'll bet you didn't even tell her about the stream."

"Oh, good grief! I forgot all about that.

The Professor's been telling us about a new discovery we—I mean, he—made."

"What's all this about a stream?" said Mrs. Dunn.

"Up in the woods," Danny explained. "You know where there's a valley in the Midston Hills, where the old logging track runs off Cowbridge Road? We always go fishing there."

"Yes, I know the stream you mean. What about it?"

"I—um—happened to taste the water this morning. It had a funny, sourish kind of taste. We wondered if there could be some kind of pollution in it."

Mrs. Dunn stood in thought for a moment and then said, "Let's look at a map. Come into the study."

This was a small room off the living room in which the walls were lined with books. There was a fireplace which made it a cosy place for reading in winter, and a desk where Mrs. Dunn kept her papers and accounts. The children followed her there. From a drawer, she took a large-scale map of the Midston area and spread it out on the desk.

"Look here," she said. "That region is north of the town. Here's the stream, this blue line. It comes from a cleft in the hills. South of it there are just woods and some houses all the way down to Route 2, and north of it there are a few farms and then the hills around Sugarloaf. There's nothing there that I know of that could cause any pollution. And the nearest factory—"

She fell silent, studying the map. "I wonder," she said.

"What, Mom?"

Mrs. Dunn put her finger on a spot some distance to the west of the stream. "This is where the Blaze factory is. Do you remember the battle we had over that place a couple of years ago?"

"I'm not sure. Something about draining the swamp?"

"That's right. Mr. Blaze wanted to drain the swamp and build his factory there because he could get the land cheaply. The Citizens' Environmental Committee opposed it. You see, wetlands like that swamp are very important. They act as a natural filter for water, underground, that supplies our wells and reservoirs. And they hold water that keeps that underground water level high. We were afraid that his factory would produce some waste material that might somehow get into the public water supply in the reservoir, once he drained the swamp. He manufactures some kind of chemicals, you know."

"I remember, now," said Danny. "You lost, didn't you?"

"Yes, we did." His mother shook her head regretfully. "Most people couldn't see any reason why a muddy old swamp shouldn't be drained off to make land for a nice, clean little factory. Mr. Blaze showed that the factory was going to be too far from the reservoir to do any harm to the public water supply. And he promised he'd filter any waste before letting it run off. So the town officials let him build the place. After all, the factory would mean jobs and money in taxes for the town."

Danny and Irene bent over the map. "It's true," Irene said. "His factory is about five miles from the reservoir, and way over on the other side of the Midston Hills."

"Yes, but I wonder whether somehow something from it isn't finding its way into that stream. I'll get in touch with one of our members, Mr. Partridge, and see if he can get a sample of the water. And we must try to get a sample of the waste that flows out of the factory." She sighed. "The trouble is that Mr. Blaze is a hard man to deal with. He has a terrible temper, and he's very stubborn. I'm afraid we're going to have trouble getting any samples from him."

She folded up the map. "Anyway, kids, thanks for telling me. It may be important."

She sat down at the desk and picked up the phone. "Close the door, will you please?" she said.

Dan and Irene went into the hall. The Professor was playing a sad and beautiful melody, and the dark notes of his bull fiddle were like melted brown sugar. In the study, they they could hear the faint clicking as Mrs. Dunn dialed a number.

Danny looked at Irene.

"A sample from the factory," he said. "Are you thinking what I'm thinking?"

4
A Day of Exploring

Joe mopped the sweat off his face with a dirty handkerchief. "Why do I let you talk me into these things?" he groaned. "I could have been lying in the shade with a book and a pitcher of lemonade."

The three friends were standing among spindly pine trees, looking out over the Midston Reservoir. It had been Irene's idea that they do some detective work, following the stream from the reservoir back up to its source before going to look at Mr. Blaze's factory.

"Let's make sure the stream does run into the reservoir, first," she said. "And then let's see whether there isn't something else higher up that could be polluting it. Otherwise, we may get into all sorts of trouble for nothing."

Danny had agreed. And so, early that morning, the three had set out on their expedition. They had biked and then walked to a spot somewhat below where they had gone fishing. They had made their way along the banks downstream, following the water. It rippled in shallow falls out of the woods at Cowbridge Road, where it passed under a bridge, then wound through open fields, and at last, having grown wider and less stony, flowed between deeper banks among the pines into the reservoir.

Danny, shading his eyes, said, "There's no doubt of it. It does end here. If there's anything bad in it, it goes into the public water supply."

"You'd think it wouldn't make much difference in all this water," said Joe, looking across the placid blue lake that lay among dark green trees.

"It depends on what the pollution is," said Irene. "And on how long it's been running into the reservoir. Look, we're right near the dam. As long as we're here—"

Joe groaned again. "More walking."

" 'Tisn't any more than a hundred yards," said Irene. "You can wait here if you want to."

"No, I'll come. It makes me feel good when you feel sorry for me."

The dam was built of concrete, and stretched in a gentle curve across the end of the reservoir. Its top was as wide as a sidewalk, and had an iron railing along it. At the far end, there was a place lower than the rest. Water was spilling over it in a steady cataract, running down the face of the dam and flowing away in a small but swiftly rushing stream in the rocky bed below. There was

a man in boots and a denim jacket standing on top of the dam smoking a cigarette. As the young people came along, he looked up and waved a hand at them.

"Can we come out on the dam and see what it looks like?" Danny called.

"Sure. Just watch your step."

They stepped from the shore to the broad concrete top and walked out to join him. From here, the dam looked much higher than it had from the side. Looking down the smooth face, they could see one or two spots where there were streaks of moisture.

Danny said, "Hey, those are cracks, aren't they? The dam is leaking."

The man laughed. "This is an oldtimer, son. It was built long before you were born. Sure, there are a couple of cracks. Old concrete always lets a little seepage through. But don't you worry, she's good for another fifty years."

"Do you work here?" Irene said.

"Yep. For the Water Company. We've been having a little trouble with the spillway gate, and I come out to look at her."

"What's a spillway gate?" Joe wanted to know.

The man motioned to the other end, where the water was running over. "That's her. A place where overflow water can run off. Under that cut-down place there's a steel gate that can be cranked down so even more water can be let out. When the reservoir is full, and if we was to have a big storm with lots more rain, we'd open that gate. That would keep water from running over the top of the dam, and lessen the pressure."

"What would happen if you didn't?" asked Danny.

"Why, too much water rushing over would make that river down there rise too high. Might even breach the top of the dam and cause a flood. There's a dozen houses further along the river, as well as the Briarly farm. They'd be mighty uncomfortable."

He chuckled and turned to gaze out over the twinkling water of the reservoir. "You know," he said, "there's three or four houses underneath this lake. Originally, there was just the river winding along quietly beside an old road. The Water Company bought the houses, put up the dam, and let the river fill the whole valley. One of the houses was an old schoolhouse with a bell on top. The say sometimes at night you can hear the bell ringing."

"Ugh! How spooky," said Irene with a shiver. "I hate to think of those empty houses under the water, and maybe the ghosts of the children who once went to that school."

"Stop," said Joe, "you're giving me day-mares."

The man looked at him quizzically, and Joe explained, "Daytime nightmares."

"Pretty good. I must remember that," said the man.

He pitched the end of his cigarette into the river below, and picked up a tool box that lay beside him. "Got to get back to work," he said. "See you later."

"Thanks a lot for telling us about everything," said Danny.

"Any time."

The three children walked back along the shore to the mouth of the stream. They made their way along it a short distance. Then Danny stopped, knelt down, and dipped up a little water in his palm.

"I just want to see if it has the same taste down here near the reservoir," he said. "Maybe it's gone."

Very gingerly, he touched his tongue to the water. He made a face. "It hasn't," he said. "In fact, it's even stronger today."

"All right, then," said Irene. "Let's go upstream as far as we can."

39

Joe sighed. "You know what we forgot?" he said. "We forgot to bring lunch."

Danny glanced at his wristwatch. "It's only a quarter to ten."

"I just thought I'd mention it."

They followed the stream back, past the spot where they had gone fishing, and for half a mile farther. The underbrush grew denser and the hills closed in. Laurel and azalea bushes clustered thickly so that it was hard to force a way through. The stream became narrower until they could jump across it easily. It was cooler here, in the shadow of the hills, but mosquitoes and deerflies began biting.

Danny stopped and looked ahead. The low, twisted branches of laurel all but blocked the way. "Let's get out of here," he said, slapping furiously at a mosquito on his neck. "We must be near the source and there's no sign of anything up this way at all."

They turned back. Half an hour later, they were on their bikes and riding toward town.

To get to the Blaze Chemical Plant meant a rather long journey around, first back to U.S. Route 2, then along it westward for a couple of miles, and then up a blacktop road to the spot where the factory stood. On the way, to quiet Joe, they stopped at a diner and had hot dogs and root beer, although it was not yet noon. Refreshed, they pedaled on and soon topped a rise and saw the factory before them.

Somewhat to their surprise, it was a neat, clean, pleasant building. It was made of brick, with lots of glass, only one story high, and not very factory-looking. There was no trace of what had once been a swamp. In front was a parking lot full of cars. A green lawn stretched on either side planted with clumps of birch trees, and behind it the woods came close. There was no fence, and Dan and his friends left their bikes in the parking lot and walked around without being disturbed.

"What are we looking for?" Joe said. "Some kind of garbage dump? Because if we are, there it is."

There was a wire fence in the rear surrounding a space where there were stacks of empty metal drums and cardboard containers. There was a truck-loading platform there, too, but its metal doors were closed.

"No," said Danny. "That's not what we want. There should be a pipe of some kind leading out to a tank. My guess is that waste water flows out the way it does in a septic system. Do you see any pipes or tanks?"

Irene shook her head and sighed. "It's probably all underground," she said. "I have a feeling we aren't going to spot it."

Dan studied the building with his chin in his hand. Then he walked purposefully toward the trees behind the factory.

"If there's anything, it would be down this way, away from the plant," he said. "It stands to reason they'd carry the water away to where they could filter it and let it run off."

A moment later, he broke into a trot. When the others caught up with him, he was pointing triumphantly at something on the very edge of the woods. It was a concrete slab some twenty feet square, with a large steel manhole cover set in it.

"I'll bet you anything this is it," Danny said. "This is the top of the filter tank. After it's filtered in here, the water must run out into a drain field somewhere further along."

Joe said, "Could be. But maybe it's just a cesspool."

Irene had walked to the other side of the slab. "I don't think so," she said. "It's leaking a bit. The ground is all wet here. And it doesn't smell like sewage."

Danny joined her. On that side, there was a good-sized puddle in a hollow next to the slab. He shoved his hands deep into his pockets and stared down at it thoughtfully.

At last, he said, "You're right. It must be stuff seeping out near the top of the tank. And if that's what it is, you know what this means?"

"Something horrible?" said Joe.

"Nope. Something good. This is what we came to find. A sample for my mother."

Irene nodded. "There's only one problem."

"What?"

"We forgot to bring a bucket. How are we going to carry some away?"

5
Dealing with
Mr. Blaze

Danny looked at Irene in dismay. Then his gaze went to the factory building on the lawn above them.

"I wonder if—" he began.

Irene shook her head firmly. "So far they haven't bothered us," she said. "But if we ask to borrow a bucket, and they want to know what it's for, we'll get into trouble. You know what your mother said about dealing with Mr. Blaze."

"I wasn't actually thinking of *asking*," Danny said reluctantly. "Just borrowing."

"That's even worse. Suppose we got caught?"

"I guess you're right."

Danny began rummaging in his pockets,

emptying out the strange and wonderful assortment of things he carried with him, figuring they might sometime come in handy. There was a coil of wire, a magnet, a sparkplug, a piece of petrified wood, an electrician's knife, a used battery from a pocket flashlight, a plastic bag folded up small, two half-inch stove bolts, a cough drop covered with pocket fluff, and a good deal more. Irene picked up the plastic bag.

"What about this?" she said, unfolding it.

It was a large, tough one which had once held a piece of electronic equipment.

Danny scratched his head. "I don't know. How can you carry a bag full of water? Maybe it would do."

Joe said suddenly, "I'll fix it. Lend me your knife."

He so seldom had any practical ideas that the other two stared at him in surprise. But Danny handed over the knife without a word.

Joe went to a large silver birch nearby. Carefully, so as not to cut too deeply into the tree, he sliced into the bark and peeled away a long strip. He rolled it into the shape of a cone and pinned it together with a few slivers of wood whittled from a twig. He punched two holes in the top and made a handle from the coil of wire. Then he took the plastic bag and put it inside this birch-bark cone, pulling the top of it out and tucking it around the edge so that it served as a lining.

"There you are," he said, handing it to Danny.

Danny and Irene had watched with their mouths hanging open. Now Dan said, "I don't believe it. Joe! You—the boy who can't even plug in a TV set without blowing all the lights out! How did you invent such a thing?"

"Oh, well," Joe said airily. "It just comes of being a genius, that's all." He snickered at the expression on their faces. "To tell you the truth, I never made one before, but I read about it once in a camping manal, and I thought it wouldn't hurt to try."

The little bucket held nearly a pint of liquid. Dan had just finished filling it from the puddle, when Irene gave him a nudge. He glanced up at her.

"Someone's coming," she said.

A man was striding down toward them from the factory. At least, he would have been striding if his legs had not been so short. He had a big, round head, broad shoulders, and a noble potbelly, and his stumpy legs trotted below trying to keep up with the rest of him, so that he looked as if he were falling downhill. He had very heavy black eyebrows, which gave him a stern look, but when he spoke his voice was not disagreeable.

"Hey, you kids," he said, "what do you think you're doing here?"

"Why—uh—we—" Danny began.

Irene put in quickly, "We're a nature-study club."

Danny looked at her in admiration. "That's right," he said. "We're collecting samples—I mean, specimens."

"Well, you should have asked permission," the man said. "This is private property."

"I'm sorry," Danny said. "We didn't think we were hurting anything."

"All right," the man said. He seemed about

to turn away, but suddenly whirled back and added, "Samples of what?"

He snapped it out so quickly that Danny answered without thinking, "This stuff that's oozing out of this tank. I guess we should have asked about it, but we were told that Mr. Blaze was kind of short-tempered."

"Is that so?" said the man. "Who told you that?"

"My moth—ouch!" said Danny. Irene had pinched him on the arm.

The man's face had become very grim. His voice, too, when next he spoke, was harsh and unpleasant. "Your mother, eh? Very interesting. Why would a boy's mother send him to grub around here in *my* woods behind *my* factory to collect samples of stuff oozing out of one of *my* tanks. That's pretty peculiar, isn't it?"

"Your factory?" Danny gulped. "Are you —are you Mr. Blaze?"

"That's right. And since you know my name, maybe you won't mind telling me yours. Or are you afraid to?"

The tone as much as the words put Danny's back up. "I'm not afraid," he said hotly. "My name's Danny Dunn."

"Just as I thought," said Mr. Blaze. His round face began to redden as if it were about to suit his name and burst into flames. "Your mother's Mrs. Dunn! That meddlesome busybody, sticking her nose into things that don't concern her! What business was it of hers where I built my factory? I took this rotten old swamp and turned it into a handsome property. My factory gives jobs to a lot of people. But if she and her ridiculous bunch of eco-nuts had had their way, I'd never have been able to do anything."

"Now, wait a minute—" said Danny.

"Wait? That's what she'd like me to do, all right, wait until doomsday. Now she sends you sneaking around here trying to find something wrong, spying on me—"

"She didn't send me," Danny put in. "And we weren't sneaking, not exactly."

"What do you mean, not exactly?" bellowed Mr. Blaze, now thoroughly roused. "That's exactly what you *were* doing. I ought to have the police after you. A nature-study club! Thought you could fool me, did you? Now get out of here. Go on, beat it!"

The three moved off without another word, trying to walk with dignity, but really rather alarmed by his anger.

"And tell your mother," Mr. Blaze shouted after them, "that if she wants to deal with me, she can get in touch with my lawyer."

"Wow!" said Joe, as they got to their bikes. "I hope I never have to see him again."

Danny got on his bike, hanging the birch-bark bucket on one side of the handlebars. He had a set, angry look of his own and all his freckles were swallowed up in a blush.

"I hope I do," he said. "I wish I could get a chance to tell him what *I* think. But he never gives you a chance to talk."

"But he was right, you know," Irene said as they began pedaling down the road away from the factory. "We were sneaking around without permission."

"I know he was right," Danny said. "That just makes it worse. Because I know he was wrong about the swamp, and about my mother's committee. And if we had asked him for permission, he would have said no anyway. Wouldn't he?"

"I suppose so," said Irene glumly. "I wish we hadn't done it, though. Maybe he'll make trouble for your mother, now."

They rode on in silence for a few minutes, and then Danny said, "Tell you what. I'll ask Professor Bullfinch what he thinks I ought to do."

"Okay," said Joe, "and while you're doing that, I'll go home and get some lunch. I haven't eaten since that hot dog about an hour ago, and I feel faint."

He left them with a wave at his corner, calling, "See you later!" Dan and Irene went on together. They turned into the driveway between their houses and stopped at Dan's kitchen door. Straddling his bike, Danny took the birch-bark bucket off the handlebars and began to say, "Let's get together after—"

Irene caught his arm. "Listen!" she said.

From the laboratory at the rear of Dan's house came a muffled shouting.

"It's the Professor's voice," Irene said with a puzzled look, "but I can't understand what he's saying."

"I can," cried Danny. "He's yelling, 'Help!' "

6
The Professor
Firmly Fixed

They let their bikes fall and darted around
to the back of the house. They pulled open
the lab door. An astonishing sight met their
eyes.

The room looked as though someone had
stirred it with a giant spoon. Glass and metal
objects were jumbled together on the surface
of one of the benches. Several pieces of equipment were stacked in a crazy pile that seemed
ready to topple over at any minute, but
miraculously didn't. Containers of plastic or
metal were stuck to the wall or to each other
on the floor. And in the center of the confusion, like a fly in a spider's web, was Professor Bullfinch.

He was bent over at an awkward angle.

His rubber apron had tools clinging to it. He wore rubber gloves, and both of them were firmly fixed to the top of the lab bench. His glasses had slipped down his nose, his hair stood wispily on end, and he looked bothered.

"Creepers!" exclaimed Danny. "What happened? Was there an explosion?"

"I suggest," said the Professor, "that we leave all explanations until I can get loose. These rubber gloves are too tight for me to pull my hands out of them. And one of my feet appears to be anchored to the floor."

Dan was still carrying the bucket, and he looked about for a safe place to put it. Since it was shaped like an ice-cream cone, it wouldn't stand up. After a moment, he hung it by its wire handle over one of the faucets in the sink, and put the plug in so that if it leaked all the liquid wouldn't be lost. Irene, meanwhile, had gone to help the Professor.

"Will I get stuck too?" she said nervously.

"No, it's all dry," said the Professor. "Just take hold of the edge of one of the gloves and peel it back so that I can get my hand free."

She did so, and the Professor drew his hand out of the rubber glove with a whistle of relief. Danny hurried over and untied the Professor's shoelace so that he could get his

foot free. The Professor peeled away the other glove, removed his rubber apron, and stepped away from the bench, rubbing his back.

"Whew! I thought no one would ever come," he said.

"How did it happen?" asked Irene.

"It was the universal glue, of course," replied the Professor. "I've been working on the problem of a container for it." He gestured at the clutter on the bench. "As you see, I haven't had much success. The trouble is that, unlike other glues, this stuff will bond to *anything* with immense strength. I have tried an immense range of materials, but it makes no difference. The stuff sticks. You might say," he added, "I'm stuck with it."

"Well, at least you aren't stuck *in* it, now," said Danny. "Can't you slow down its action so that it doesn't stick right away?"

"I've already worked out a way to slow the adhesive action," said the Professor. "But that doesn't really solve the basic problem of what to keep it in."

"I'm sure you'll think of something," Irene said comfortingly. "Meanwhile, we can help you clean up some of this mess."

She picked up something that looked like a piece of modern sculpture. It consisted of a small aluminum can, a plastic jug, a pair of pliers, a fountain pen, a glass test tube, and a coffee cup, all firmly fastened together. She looked at it doubtfully, with her head on one side.

"The question is, how can we put any of it away without getting it apart?" she said.

"Oh, just throw it all into that big wastebasket in the corner," said the Professor sadly.

"Too bad," said Danny. "If we could only unstick it, we could save that stuff. I don't think Mom's going to like having that coffee cup thrown away."

He snapped his fingers. "Listen, Professor, you told us the glue bonds to the molecules of water that cover nearly everything. If that's so, why can't we evaporate the water?"

He didn't wait for an answer. He seized one of the lighted Bunsen burners on the bench and held its blue gas flame next to the place where the coffee cup was stuck to the plastic jug. He turned the valve so that the flame shot out, hissing strongly. There was a *pop!* and half of the plastic jug disappeared, leaving a terrible smell behind. The coffee cup cracked across, and one piece tinkled to the floor.

"Oh, gosh," said Danny.

"Shut off the burner," said the Professor

rather wearily. "I do wish, Dan, that you'd think before diving headfirst into these things. Say, 'Whoa,' to yourself, or count up to ten. No, maybe a hundred would be better."

"But Professor Bullfinch," said Irene. "Danny's just given you the answer. You ought to thank him."

"The answer? To counting up to a hundred?"

"No, no. The answer to the problem of what to put the glue in. Don't you see?"

Professor Bullfinch looked at her in bafflement. "All I see is a melted plastic jug and a broken coffee cup, my dear. Surely you don't mean those?"

"No, no, no!" cried Irene. "Evaporation! Think about it. Isn't Danny right?"

The Professor took off his glasses and looked at them thoughtfully, as if he was staring himself in the face.

"Goodness!" he said. "Of course. It shows you—you can be too close to a problem sometimes, so that even though the solution is right there you don't see it."

He put his glasses back on. "Mind you, it is far from easy. It is very, *very* hard to get that last thin monolayer of water off things. It requires expensive equipment and a hard vacuum, something like that of outer space.

But luckily, Midston University has the proper equipment, and I'm sure I can use it. If I were to burn all the moisture out of a container first, I could then seal the glue into it."

"You'd have to work fast, though," said Danny. "And how would you get the glue out again?"

"I'd put a valve of some sort on the container. I'd shoot the glue out under pressure and the valve would seal up immediately after it. Excellent," the Professor said, with satisfaction. "I think I must show my gratitude by naming the new glue after both of you."

"Not me," Danny said. "Not after what I did. It was really Irene who made you see what should be done. Name it after her."

"Right! I will call it *Irenium*."

Irene blushed. "It's a big honor, but I don't really deserve it."

The door opened. Mrs. Dunn peered into the lab, and said, "Is everyone in here deaf?"

"I don't think so," said the Professor. "Have you been knocking long?"

"I've been blowing the car horn, and shouting, and generally losing my temper. There are two bikes lying in the driveway directly in front of the kitchen door, and I have a car full of groceries which I don't feel like lugging around them."

"Sorry, Mom," said Danny. "We'll get them out of your way and help you with the groceries. We had to help the Professor, who was all stuck together."

Mrs. Dunn raised her eyebrows. "Stuck together? I should hope so. I wouldn't like to see him lying around in pieces."

Her gaze went past Danny to the confusion on the lab bench. "Ah, I understand. That new glue I've been hearing about. Is that one of my Worcester coffee cups I see with a piece out of it?"

"It was an accident," Danny said.

"Ah, well, I can think of it as a sacrifice to the march of science," said Mrs. Dunn. "Come on, let's get the groceries in. And Professor, you'd better do something about that shoe or your foot may catch cold."

The children hastened to help her, while Professor Bullfinch got to work on his clean-up job. Not until the last of the groceries were stowed on the kitchen counter did Danny remember his expedition of the morning.

"I wanted to talk to you about Mr. Blaze, Mom," he said.

"Oh, yes, so did I," said Mrs. Dunn. She

was stacking cans in the cupboard, and she straightened and pushed a lock of hair out of her eyes with the back of a hand. "I mean, so did I want to talk to you. About that stream you were fishing in and the funny taste of the water."

"Did you find out anything?"

"Yes, we certainly did. I asked Mr. Partridge if he knew where the stream was, and he said he did, because he went fishing there now and then, so I asked him to get a sample of the water. Another of our members had it analyzed."

"And was there some pollution in it, Mrs. Dunn?" Irene said.

"Yes, in a way. It depends on what you call pollution. There was something in it—just a minute, I have it written down on a piece of paper." She got her purse and dug through it, muttering, "I have almost as much in here as Danny has in his pockets. Ah, here we are, here's the note I made. It's an organic sulfate salt, whatever that is. According to the chemist who analyzed it, it's a rare one, one he isn't familiar with."

"Then it must come from Mr. Blaze's factory," said Danny positively.

Mrs. Dunn shook her head. "We don't know that for sure, yet. Anyway, this salt is harmless, the chemist thinks, although since it's rare it's hard to say what it might do. A lot more testing would be needed. Our next step is to prove that it's the same as the waste material from the Blaze plant."

Danny took a deep breath. "I've got a sample for you," he said.

Mrs. Dunn straightened slowly and stared at her son. "Danny," she said, in a What-Have-You-Been-Up-To-Now? voice.

Danny began to wonder if what had seemed like such a good idea was really such a good idea after all. However, he plunged on bravely. "We went up to Mr. Blaze's factory today and got it."

"We?" Mrs. Dunn's eyes went to Irene, who turned pink. "Yes, of course. And Joe, too, I suppose. You'd better tell me about it. I don't imagine Mr. Blaze gave you the sample because he liked your looks."

"Well, no . . . he didn't." Danny swallowed hard. "He didn't really like our taking it. In fact, he kicked us off his property. But you said you wished you could get a sample, and that he was a hard man to deal with, and I thought we'd just try to help out."

"Oh, Danny! Well, go on." Mrs. Dunn was curious in spite of herself. "You didn't break into his factory, did you?"

" 'Course not. We looked around outside and found what I figured was the outflow tank down near the woods. Some stuff had leaked out of it and was just lying there in a puddle on the surface. Joe had this great idea for how to make a bucket out of birch-bark, and we scooped some up. Then Mr. Blaze caught us and—uh—well—he yelled at us a little and then told us to go."

"I see. It might have been worse." She ran her hand through her hair, which was as fiery as Danny's. Then, struck by another thought, she said, "Did he ask you who you were?"

In a small voice, Danny said, "Yes."

Mrs. Dunn stared out the kitchen window for a long moment while she tried to control herself. Then she said, "That's not going to do our Citizens' Committee much good, I'm afraid."

"Gosh, I'm sorry, Mom, I really am. I just thought I'd be able to help," Danny said.

"I know." She drummed her fingers on the counter. "Next time you have a marvelous idea like that, I wish you'd come and ask me first. Where's this sample, now?"

"I left it in the lab. Do you want me to get it?"

"No. In the first place, you don't know for sure it's really the waste from his factory, do you? You just found a tank with some liquid running out of it. It wasn't labeled, was it? It might have been sewage."

"It wasn't sewage, Mrs. Dunn," Irene said.

"Maybe not, but you don't know what it was. If we're going to make a case, we have to have an official sample. And now that we know there is some kind of chemical in that stream, we are going to have another hearing, and we'll be able to force Mr. Blaze to produce a sample of the waste from his plant. If you had only waited——!" She shook her head. "Now, it's going to be very difficult for me to face Mr. Blaze. Heaven knows what I'll say to him."

She looked at her son, and at Irene. They were staring at her wide-eyed and uncomfortable.

"Oh, well, never mind," she said. "You acted for the best and maybe it will be all right. Goodness! Look how late it is. Let's get these things put away, and see whether we can find anything to eat. I haven't had my lunch, yet, and I'm as hungry as—as—as a Joe Pearson!"

7
"I accuse—
her!"

"Stormy weather," said the radio newscaster cheerfully, several days later. "A storm center moving slowly from the northwest has already caused flash floods in some states. . . . We can expect thunderstorms and heavy rain with winds around thirty miles an hour. . . . Should reach here in the next twelve hours. Unpack your umbrellas."

"You'd never guess it," Danny said, looking up from his breakfast and out the kitchen window. The sky was clear and blue, the air still and warm.

"Yes, but that weather report describes today, all right," said Mrs. Dunn. "We're having our meeting with Mr. Blaze this morning. Right now, everything's quiet, but in a few hours there'll be stormy weather when that meeting starts."

She turned off the radio. "I'd better get my notes in order. I'm waiting to hear from Mrs. Newman about the time of the meeting."

"Can I come, Mom?" Danny asked. "I'd like to listen to what goes on."

"I don't see why not. It's a public hearing. And after all, you're responsible for it. You found out that the stream had the chemical in it."

"What about—"

"Joe and Irene? I'm pretty sure Professor and Mrs. Miller will be there, and Mrs. Pearson, too, although Mr. Pearson can't get away."

She went off to her study and Danny attacked his bacon and eggs again. He was washing his dishes, when Professor Bullfinch came in holding a metal container about the size of a can of beans in one hand, and a coffee cup in the other.

"Good morning," Danny said. "Have you had your breakfast?"

"Oh," said the Professor, "I knew I'd forgotten something. I started very early in the lab this morning."

"I'll make some for you," Danny said.

"And there's lots of coffee on the stove. I see you brought your own cup."

The Professor held it up. "It'll make your mother happy. It's the one that was broken the other day. I couldn't fix it until I'd sorted out the problem of a container for the Irenium."

"Is that it—that can?"

"It is. As you see, it has a nozzle with a valve through which the glue feeds under high pressure."

"That's great. How do you want your eggs?"

"Scrambled, please." The Professor poured some coffee into the mended cup and inspected it for leaks. Then he happily gulped down a mouthful. "Where is your mother, my boy? I want to see if she has anything else to be repaired. I'd like to try this out."

"In her study. I'll go tell her you want to experiment with your glue on some of her things."

"Um—I wouldn't put it like that, Danny," said the Professor. "She might get the wrong idea."

Danny put a dish of smoking scrambled eggs on the table, and while the Professor ate, went to find his mother. He stopped at the door of the study, for Mrs. Dunn was talking on the phone.

"At eleven?" she was saying. "All right, Dorothy. I'll meet you and Monroe there. What? Yes, I know—I don't mind telling you I wish something would happen to Mr. Blaze to keep him from showing up. I know he's going to shout and carry on like anything. His lawyer is so much easier to talk to. Yes, I know, it's like asking for a miracle. All right, see you later. Bye-bye."

She hung up and glanced quizzically at Danny. He gave her the Professor's message, and then went upstairs to his own room to work at the citizens band scanner he was making from a kit.

But he couldn't keep his mind off the telephone conversation he had just heard. He knew it was none of his business, and yet he couldn't help wondering if there was any way of keeping Mr. Blaze away from the meeting. He told himself that he'd only get into trouble again, but his was the kind of mind that couldn't leave a problem without trying to solve it. And he did want his mother's committee to have the best possible chances of winning.

He turned back to his work, but at last put down the screwdriver and sat with his chin on his palms, his elbows propped on the desk.

"If I could just get a really good solution, I'd keep it a secret," he said to himself. "Something that really wouldn't hurt anybody. And if it worked, I wouldn't even mind getting into trouble as long as I could keep everybody else from getting all gummed up in it with me. I wouldn't tell—"

He paused, staring at the wall, for with the words an idea had formed in his head. He thought about it for a long time, and a big grin spread across his face.

"I'll do it!" he said. And, as was usually the case when he had what seemed like a good idea, he stopped thinking about it and enthusiastically decided to put it into action at once.

He jumped up and ran downstairs. Mrs. Dunn was still in her study.

"When's that meeting, Mom?" he asked.

"At eleven, dear."

"Where?"

"At the Town Hall."

"Okay, I'll meet you there."

Mrs. Dunn nodded, busy with her notes.

Dan went to the kitchen phone and called Irene and then Joe, telling them both about the meeting and explaining that he had some work to do but would meet them at the Town Hall. Then he went into the lab. The Professor was in his small office, writing busily in a notebook.

"Professor, I wonder if I could borrow that can of Irenium?" Danny said.

"Why? Have you something to repair?" said the Professor without looking up.

"Well—er—in a way. There's something I want to fix." It was the truth, after all, he told himself, because he wanted to fix the meeting so that his mother's committee wouldn't have to argue with Mr. Blaze.

The Professor said, "It's on the lab bench, Dan. Put it back when you're finished."

A few minutes later, Danny was on his bike and speeding up Elm Street toward U.S. Route 2. As he approached the corner where the Midston Sweete Shoppe was, he saw Eddie Phillips just getting on his bike in front of the store. Danny had to stop for the traffic light, and Eddie said, "What's in the can? More fish dynamite?"

"Bug killer for pests like you," Dan replied.

"Wise guy."

The light changed, and Danny took off. If he had glanced over his shoulder he would have seen Eddie swing his own bike around and begin following him at a distance. But he was so full of his plan that he never gave another thought either to Eddie or to the fact that the other boy's nickname was Snitcher.

At a quarter to eleven, the big room in the Town Hall that was used for public meetings was more than half-full. A lot of people in Midston belonged to the Citizens' Environmental Committee, and even those who didn't were concerned about a problem as serious as this. Although many people had to work, quite a few had been able to get to the meeting. Mrs. Dunn, who was president of the committee, sat in the front row with two other officers, Mr. Partridge and Mrs. Newman. Irene and Joe were in the row behind her, with Irene's parents, Mrs. Pearson, and Professor Bullfinch. But there was no sign of Danny.

"Where do you suppose he is?" Irene whispered to Joe.

"I don't know. All he told me was that he had some work to do. Maybe it was something for his mother."

The mayor, Mr. Narciso, had taken his seat at a long table at one end of the room. With him were the members of the Town Council. He glanced at his wristwatch and picked up his gavel.

"It's nearly eleven," he said. "Mr. Starling, is your client here yet?"

Mr. Starling was Mr. Blaze's lawyer. He also sat in the front row, but at the other end from the members of the Citizens' Committee. He was a plump man with gold-rimmed glasses and a smooth, round face. He had a smooth, round way of talking, too, never using a simple word if he could find a more complicated one.

He said, "I regret to say he has not yet arrived. However, I am certain he will effect an appearance momentarily."

"Well," said Mr. Narciso, "I'd like to start on time. This was supposed to be an open meeting, but I didn't expect so many people, and if we get into long discussions we'll be here all day."

"May I ask for a brief delay, sir? I will telephone him from the hall."

"Go ahead, then."

As Mr. Starling got up, Danny slipped quietly into the aisle seat Joe had been holding for him.

"Where've you been?" Joe demanded.

"Oh—around. Tell you later. What's happening?"

"Mr. Blaze hasn't turned up yet," Joe said.

"Is that so?" Danny said innocently. "I wonder what happened to him?"

Mrs. Dunn turned around and smiled at him. She put her finger on her lips, for Mr. Starling had come back.

"He departed from his office ten minutes ago," Mr. Starling said. "Perhaps excessive traffic has caused him to be delayed."

"Hmph! I'll give him another five minutes," said Mr. Narciso.

Everyone relaxed, and people began talking and shifting around in their seats. After a time, Mrs. Dunn looked at her watch, showed it to Mrs. Newman, and held up her crossed fingers.

Mrs. Newman said, "Somebody must have heard you when you asked for a miracle."

Joe, sitting behind her, scratched his head and began muttering to himself.

"What are you saying?" Irene asked.

"I'm trying to find a rhyme for 'miracle,' " said Joe.

"There isn't one, is there?" said Danny.

"Sure there is. There's a rhyme for almost any word—except 'orange.' For instance, there's 'lyrical,' 'satirical,' and—and— 'spiracle.' "

" 'Spiracle'? What's that?"

"It's the hole in the top of a whale's head, the opening he spouts through," said Irene. "How could you use that in a poem?"

Joe thought for a second, and said,

> It would be something of a miracle,
> If Mr. Narciso sneezed through his
> spiracle.

The other two spluttered with laughter, and Irene said, "How does he do it?"

They were interrupted by the rapping of Mr. Narciso's gavel.

"All right, ladies and gentlemen," the mayor said. "It's a quarter past eleven. Let's get started. It isn't fair to hold everyone up. It's obvious Mr. Blaze isn't coming."

"Oh, yes he is!" roared a voice from the back of the hall.

All the heads swiveled around together to look. It was a sight worth looking at.

Mr. Blaze stood there in a rage. His big head was thrust forward, his heavy eyebrows bristling over his snapping eyes. But he wore no trousers. Instead, he had a gay plaid blanket wrapped around his waist and fastened with a belt. He looked like a Scotsman in a kilt far too big for him.

As everyone stared, he waddled down the center aisle, almost tripping over the flapping blanket. When he got to where his lawyer was sitting, he stopped.

"A plot!" he cried. "A pants plot to keep me from getting here. And I accuse—her!"

He shot out his hand and pointed straight at Mrs. Dunn.

8
The Meeting

For a moment, everyone sat in stunned silence. Then Mr. Narciso said uncertainly, "I don't get this. Are you saying that Mrs. Dunn stole your trousers?"

That broke the tension and everyone began to laugh. Everyone except Mrs. Dunn. She got to her feet and said, "Mr. Blaze, that's not true. You're simply trying to break up the meeting. I've been right here. However you lost your pants, you know perfectly well I had nothing to do with it."

"Oh, no?" shouted Mr. Blaze. "Is that so? Well, I can prove it!"

Mr. Narciso hammered the desk with his gavel. "Order!" he said. "Quiet!" And when everyone had more or less settled down again, he went on, "All right, Mr. Blaze. Suppose you explain yourself."

"Sure," Mr. Blaze said, more quietly. "I left my factory about half an hour ago. I got here before eleven and parked my car out in the parking lot. Then I tried to get out. I couldn't."

"What do you mean, you couldn't? Were you paralyzed?" said Mr. Narciso. "Or did you discover you weren't wearing any pants?"

"I was wearing them, all right," snarled Mr. Blaze. "But they were stuck to the car seat. I couldn't believe it, but there I was, stuck fast. I was behind the steering wheel, so I couldn't get them off. I just couldn't move."

Some people stared, others tittered, some whispered.

"I'd have been there yet," Mr. Blaze continued, "except that a nice kid came along and loaned me his scout knife. I had to cut my pants open to get out of them and off the seat. Luckily, I had a blanket in the car. A perfectly good pair of trousers ruined! They're still there, sticking to the car seat—what's left of them."

By this time, the Professor, Joe, and Irene were all looking at Danny. Danny gazed helplessly at Mr. Blaze, and his face was the color of a beautiful sunset over the Rockies.

"What's more," Mr. Blaze said, "that same kid who helped me told me he knew who did it. He followed another boy who biked out to my factory this morning, stopped at my car with some kind of can in his hand, and then biked back to town. The kid—his name's Eddie Phillips—"

"Snitcher!" said Joe.

"—followed the other boy back and saw him come into the Town Hall."

"What?" said Mr. Narciso. "Is he here now?"

"Yes, he is. His name's Danny Dunn. There he sits."

A babble broke out, over which rose the pounding of Mr. Narciso's gavel. But Mr. Blaze's voice rose still louder.

"There's your proof," he said. "He's Mrs. Dunn's son. It's obvious she sent him to keep me from getting to this meeting so she and her people could stop me from having a fair hearing."

"That's not true!" Danny leaped to his feet and ran down the aisle. He stopped before Mr. Narciso's table.

Mr. Narciso banged once more with his

gavel, but everyone was silent already, waiting to hear what the boy would say.

"Sure, I did it," Danny said. "I used a new kind of glue Professor Bullfinch invented. I did want to keep Mr. Blaze from coming to the meeting, because he's so short-tempered that he yells at people instead of listening to them."

There was some sympathetic laughter, and Mr. Blaze looked as though he were about to explode again, but Mr. Starling pulled him down into a seat.

"I thought it wouldn't do any harm, because his lawyer would be here," Danny said. "I know it was wrong and I shouldn't have done it, but I got excited by the idea and I just didn't stop to think things all the way through. Everybody says that about me, and they're right." He looked squarely at Mr. Narciso. "But I promise you nobody else knew about it. Not my mother, not Professor Bullfinch, not even my best friends. Nobody. I did it all on my own. And I've got eleven dollars in my savings bank and I'll give it to Mr. Blaze to pay for his pants."

Mr. Narcisco's lips twitched, and he put up a hand to cover a smile. Then he said gravely, "I believe you, Dan."

"Rubbish!" said Mr. Blaze. "A pack of lies!"

Mr. Narciso regarded him coldly. "I don't think so. If you don't mind my saying so, Mr. Blaze, you're a newcomer here in Midston. But Mrs. Dunn has been a neighbor of ours for a long time, and I've known this boy almost from the time he was born. Just as he says, he tends to get into mischief, and he's bull-headed and thoughtless, but I don't think he's a liar."

He turned to Dan. "That doesn't make what you did right. I'll leave it to your Ma to decide what to do about that. Meanwhile, go sit down and we'll get on with this meeting."

Danny returned to his seat. His mother gave him one look, both angry and sad, which made his heart sink. Even Professor Bullfinch shook his head. But when the meeting began and nobody was looking, Irene patted Danny's arm, and Joe whispered to him, "Never mind. If they put you in jail, I'll send you a cake with a file in it."

Mr. Narciso was saying, "I give the floor to Mrs. Dunn, President of the Citizen's Environmental Committee."

Mrs. Dunn stood up, holding some papers. "I'm sorry about that interruption," she said.

"I apologize for my son. Now, I won't go into the whole history of the Blaze Rare Chemical Company. We are all familiar with it. However, our committee has asked for this meeting because some new information has come to light. I have here a relief map of the town land." She handed it over to Mr. Narciso, who spread it out on the table so the other council members could look at it. "As you see, there is a stream which begins in the Midston Hills at the spot we have marked *A* and runs down for a distance of approximately a mile and three-quarters, passing under Cowbridge Road and entering the Midston Reservoir at the spot we have marked *B*.

"That stream now contains some foreign material consisting of an organic sulfate salt. Here is the chemical analysis of it, made by the Siegel Chemical Laboratory."

She passed over another paper, and went on. "I have here a chemical analysis of a sample of waste liquid which is discharged by the Blaze Rare Chemical Company. This sample was furnished to us by the company and analyzed by the Siegel Laboratory, too. As you can see, it contains the same material."

Mr. Narciso took the third paper and,

after looking at it, passed it around to the councilors.

He said, "Have you got any explanation for how that stuff is getting from the factory all the way over to that stream? They're two or three miles apart and separated by hills."

Mrs. Dunn nodded. "When the whole matter of draining Boardman's Swamp came up two years ago, for the building of the factory, we pointed out that the land is part of the watershed. The swamp held surface water that filtered down into the water table, and there is an underground stream that can be traced in that area which connects with several streams and which feeds the stream we're talking about. They're all marked in blue on the map. You can't separate one part of the water table from another—all that water eventually flows down to the reservoir and then to the sea. It's all the same water."

One of the council members, Miss Weiss, put in, "What's Mr. Blaze got to say about this? Isn't he supposed to have a filtering system out there at the factory?"

Mr. Blaze started to get up, but his lawyer caught his arm, said something to him in a low tone, and got up in his place.

"You are quite right," Mr. Starling said

in his smooth, soft voice. "The plant has a perfectly adequate filtration system and the complete plans for it are on file with the Inspection Department. It is possible that a small quantity of the sulfate is finding its way into the reservoir. But the material is absolutely harmless."

He opened his briefcase and took out a small bottle. "I have here," he said, "three ounces of water containing the same proportion of the sulfate salt which might appear in the reservoir." He unscrewed the top and drank the contents of the bottle. He looked around with a satisfied air and said. "There you are. We've all been drinking the reservoir water with this material in it, and none of us has suffered any ill consequences, any more than I have."

Mrs. Dunn said dryly, "That's a very dramatic demonstration, but it doesn't prove a thing. I understand that the stuff is a rare substance and not much is known about it—"

"It's nothing more than a kind of detergent, such as you might wash your dishes in, madam," said Mr. Starling.

"Maybe so. I'd like to remind you that people have been putting chlorine into drinking water to purify it for years, but only recently they've discovered that the chlorine reacts with organic matter in the water to form chloroform, which *is* dangerous to people's health. People used to argue that DDT was safe, too, and it took time to find out that it passed into the food chain and was dangerous. We're just asking you not be in such a hurry. We're asking for you to stop production for a while, until some more extensive tests can be made. Let's try to find out some more about this stuff."

"Mrs. Dunn doesn't know much about factories or business, that's clear," Mr. Blaze cried, starting to his feet in spite of all Mr. Starling could do to keep him quiet. "We've got fifty people working at the plant. They'll all be without jobs, just because a bunch of environmental nuts are scared of their shadows. My factory pays a lot of money to the town in taxes. Do you want to drive me out of business? And what about all those people working for me—your own neighbors?"

Mr. Partridge, the vice-president of the Citizens' Environmental Committee, said, "The mistake was made back in the beginning when the town was rushed into letting the swamp be drained. All we're saying now is, let's not be rushed into anything else. Maybe Mr. Blaze can put in a new filtering system that will take all this pollution out of his waste."

"That would cost a fortune!" fumed Mr. Blaze. "And it isn't pollution. You can eat it with a spoon without getting anything more serious than a bellyache."

Mr. Partridge was a big, slow-moving man, but when he was angry his voice was like the roar of a bear. It roared out now, drowning even Mr. Blaze. "I don't want bellyaches just because you're stingy!"

"All right, let's calm down," said Mr. Narciso. "I recognize Mr. Quill."

Mr. Quill was the oldest member of the Town Council. He had been elected every term for as long as anyone could remember, so that some people said he had gone to the council when he was a boy instead of going to school. He was well known for finding ways to stop arguments.

He said, "I'd like to make a motion which I think can settle this whole matter. I move that we allow Mr. Blaze to continue production. As he says, we don't want to put him out of business, and the stuff seems harmless enough. But at the same time, I move we appoint a committee to investigate this what-chamacallit—salt of whatever it is that's getting into the reservoir—and make a report back to us on it in a month."

"A month! That's hardly enough time," said Mrs. Dunn.

"It's a start," said Mr. Quill.

"Okay," said Mr. Narciso. "This is now a matter for the council to debate. Any discussion?"

The council members shook their heads.

"We'll vote on it, then. All those in favor?"

All the town councilors raised their hands.

"Carried unanimously," said Mr. Narciso. "Meeting's adjourned."

9
Danny
in Disgrace

Mrs. Dunn, Professor Bullfinch, and Danny drove home together in silence. Danny wriggled uncomfortably in the back seat, wishing he had the power to flip the days over like the pages of a calendar so that it could be next week, with everything that had happened and was going to happen already over and done with.

When they were home, and in the kitchen, Mrs. Dunn said, "Danny, I'm not going to waste time scolding you. You know that what you did was wrong and you know why it was wrong. But—what on earth am I going to do with you? You jump from one hasty, headstrong act into another. You just never seem to think."

She sank down on a chair, shaking her head.

Danny bit his lip, feeling almost ready to cry. "Gosh, what can I say?" he protested. "I said I was sorry. I'll try not to do it again."

"After all, my dear Mrs. Dunn," said the Professor, gently, "he thought he was acting for the best. Lots of us do the same and find that we've made mistakes. Only many of us don't own up to them in public the way Danny did."

"And I meant what I said," Danny added. "I'll send Mr. Blaze everything I have in my savings account."

Mrs. Dunn couldn't help a smile, but she quickly became serious again. "I'm afraid you'll find that Mr. Blaze's trousers cost a lot more than eleven dollars. You'll have to give up your allowance every week for as long as it takes to pay for them."

"All right."

"And you'll apologize to Mr. Blaze."

Danny swallowed hard. "You mean, I have to go see him? He won't listen to me. He'll just holler."

"Well . . ." Mrs. Dunn relented a trifle. "You can write to him." So as soon as lunch was finished, Dan sat down and wrote a note:

Dear Mr. Blaze, I know it was wrong to glue your pants to the car seat and I apologize. I hope you will excuse me. I enclose $11 for part of the payment for your pants and please tell me how much the rest is and I'll pay it back to you when I get my allowance.

Yours truly,
Danny Dunn

Then he biked down to the bank, drew out his savings, put them into the envelope with the letter, and mailed them off. That made him feel a little better.

But as he was coming out of the post office, he passed two people going in. They grinned at him, and behind his back he heard one say, "Yeah, that's the kid who did it," and then they both laughed. He could feel his cheeks grow hot. He jumped on his bike and pedaled off, sure that everyone was pointing at him and talking about him.

The day had begun to match his gloomy mood. Flat-topped clouds were boiling up out of the west, the blue of the sky was graying, and the air seemed to press down on him heavily. Somewhere, far off, thunder bumped. When he got home, the house was empty. His mother had left a note on the kitchen bulletin board saying: "I may be back late.

If so, feed yourselves. There's a casserole in the oven: 25 min. at 350°." He prowled out to the laboratory, but the Professor had gone out, too.

The way he was feeling, Danny was just as happy to be alone. He perched himself on a stool at one of the lab benches, and stared out at the lawn and garden. It seemed as though, for the past few weeks, he could do nothing right.

"Why am I the way I am?" he mumbled to himself. "I have these great ideas and then *foof!* they blow up in my face. What I need is a special kind of control, like what they put on engines to keep them from going too fast. A safety catch, maybe, so that when I got an idea I'd be stopped from doing anything."

He picked up a pencil and began doodling on a scrap of paper, drawing circuits and switches.

"The way it would work," he said to himself, beginning to get interested in spite of his misery, "is, I'd have a machine mounted on me somewhere that would monitor my blood pressure, heartbeat, and maybe my brain waves. Then, see, when I got a really exciting idea and my heart started to pound and my brain got active, the machine would pick that up. It would send a shortwave signal that would set off an alarm. Let's see . . . I'd have to have the alarm set in Mom's ear, like a hearing aid—"

He became aware of a steady knocking sound. He pulled his mind away from what he was doing and brought his eyes into focus. Joe was standing outside tapping on the window. Irene was with him. When she saw that he was looking, she mouthed the words "Can we come in?"

For a minute, he almost said no. But puzzling over his new invention had raised his spirits again, and he found that he felt much better. He beckoned to them. They went around to the door.

"What happened?" Irene said as they entered. "Did she blow up at you?"

"Not much," said Danny. "There wasn't much she could say that I didn't already know, was there?"

"I guess not. Oh, Danny! How could you do such a crazy thing?"

"Don't you start on him," said Joe. "And anyway, you've got to admit it was pretty funny when Mr. Blaze came in looking like himself on top and somebody's grandmother on the bottom."

"It was funny," said Irene. "But not for Mr. Blaze."

"Well, I wrote him an apology and sent him my money," Danny said. "I'm going to have to send him a lot more, too. I wonder how much men's pants *do* cost?"

"How did you know which car was his?" said Joe.

"Well, when we were first out there, at the factory, you know we left our bikes in the parking lot. There was one section of the lot which had spaces reserved for company officials, and one space was marked *J. R. Blaze*. So the car in that spot had to be his."

"Neat!" said Joe.

Irene said, "Well, anyway, something good came out of it. You got the sample of waste from the factory for your mother."

"Oh—that. Didn't you hear what she said?" Danny replied. "She never even used it. Her committee got their own official sample from the plant."

He kicked moodily at the leg of the bench. "All I did was get us a pack of trouble. If anything good came out of that trip to the factory it was that Joe made that great birch-bark bucket."

"That's right," Joe said. "When you threw the sample away, I hope you didn't throw the bucket out, too. I'd like to have it. It's the only way I can prove I once invented something."

"I never threw the sample out," Dan said. "My mother told me she wouldn't need it and I forgot all about it. I left it right here in the lab, somewhere. But where?"

He ran his fingers through his hair, trying to remember. "I came rushing in— the Professor was over there—oh, yeah! I remember. I hung it on the faucet of the sink."

It was still there. He started to lift it off, and hesitated.

"Funny," he said. "It's empty."

"The Professor must have emptied it out," said Joe.

"He wouldn't do that," Danny said. "He'd have guessed from the bark bucket that it was something of ours, and he'd never do anything with it without asking me first."

He bent over the sink. "No, it's simple," he said. "It just leaked out of the bottom of the bucket. But where did it go? I remember, I put the stopper in the drain so that if this happened the stuff wouldn't be lost, and I could just scoop it out of the sink. But the sink's empty, too."

"Well, maybe the stopper wasn't in tightly enough," Irene suggested.

"No," said Danny. "That's not it."

There was something in his tone that made Irene look twice at him. "What do you mean?" she said.

Solemnly, he crooked a finger at her. She and Joe went over to join him. Wordlessly, he pointed to the bottom of the sink.

There was a long crack in the concrete of which the sink was made.

Still silent, Danny knelt down and examined the floor underneath the sink. Then his finger stabbed out again. There was another crack, a smaller one, directly under the sink. But of the liquid from the bucket there was no trace at all.

10
Funny Coincidences

"What a funny coincidence!" said Irene. "But still, it doesn't matter, does it? I mean, you don't need the stuff anymore. And even if there hadn't been a crack in the floor, it would have evaporated by now, anyway."

Joe carefully lifted the birch-bark bucket off the faucet and examined it with admiration. "Did I really make this?" he said. "Wow! I'm good."

"You can use it for 'Show and Tell' when you get to college," Irene remarked.

"You're just jealous," Joe said smugly. "Listen, what'll we do this afternoon?"

"Nothing outside," said Irene. 'It's getting real dark. It's going to pour pretty soon."

She glanced at Danny. He had said nothing, but was standing with his head down, his hands in his pockets, staring at the floor.

"Danny, quit sulking," she said. "We know you feel bad about what happened this morning, but it's all over. We understand why you did it, and so do all your friends. You've got to snap out of it."

He raised his head. His blue eyes had a faraway look in them. "I'm not sulking," he said. "I'm not even thinking about what happened this morning. It's something else."

"What else?"

"Funny coincidences."

He leaned back against the stone-topped bench, and after a minute, during which both Joe and Irene waited in bewilderment, he went on. "Listen. The sink is made out of concrete, right? There was no crack in it before. I know that, because I'd have seen one when I put the stopper in. Now, suddenly, there's a crack so that all the stuff leaked out.

"Number two: the floor is made of concrete. And suddenly a crack appears right under the sink, so that when the stuff leaked out of the sink, it leaked away through the floor, too."

"I don't get you," said Joe. "Are you trying to say somebody crept in here and made those cracks?"

"Just a minute. One more point. Where did we get that sample from in the first place?"

"You know that as well as we do. From the ground next to the filter tank at Mr. Blaze's factory. Why?"

"Don't you remember that tank? It was made of concrete," said Dan.

Irene put her hands to her cheeks, frowning in thought.

Joe said, "Termites! Concrete-eating termites!"

Irene glanced sideways at him and made a face. She said, "I see what you mean, Danny. Why was there a puddle of liquid next to the factory filter tank? It must have leaked out. Something made it leak out of that tank, and then leak out of the sink here, and then leak through the floor. Something—oh!"

"Right," Danny said grimly. "Now you get it. The stuff itself! There's something in that liquid that eats right through concrete."

As if to punctuate his words, there came a low growl of thunder.

Irene walked to the window and stared out at the darkening sky. "It sounds too weird to be true. How can it do that? And if it does, why doesn't it eat right through people?"

"I don't know," Danny confessed. "But

can you think of another explanation for all the facts?"

"If only we had some more of the stuff," said Irene. "We could experiment with it and make sure."

Danny snapped his fingers. "There's another way we can make sure. Go home and get your raincoat. I'll get mine. We'll bike past Joe's place and let him get his."

"Wait a minute, wait a minute, *wait a minute!*" Joe screeched. "I don't know what you're talking about. What have raincoats got to do with experimenting and eating concrete? I don't want to eat concrete. I don't need a raincoat—"

"Yes, you do," said Danny, "if you want to come with us."

"I don't even know where you're going. How do I know if I want to come there? Maybe it's someplace horrible."

"You'll find out," Danny said. "Go on, Irene. I'll meet you outside."

Instead of moving, Irene grabbed him by the shoulders and shook him. "No!" she said. "You wait just a minute. We're not going to go charging off with you again until you tell us what you're thinking of. You just finished one piece of trouble and now you're going to jump into another. It's going to be something like—like—going back to the Blaze factory or getting us all arrested."

"Nothing like that," Danny retorted. "I just want to take you to a place where there's some concrete and some of that sulfate salt solution. Nowhere near the Blaze factory. Nowhere that'll get us into trouble. I swear it! If you don't want to come with me, I'm going by myself. Only it would be better if I had witnesses."

Irene wrinkled up her nose. "Oh, all right," she said. "I'll meet you in the driveway in five minutes."

"Three minutes," said Danny.

It was actually only about two minutes later that the three set out on their bikes. They sped to Jefferson Street, where Joe lived, and he got his raincoat and left his birch-bark bucket at home. Then, with Danny in the lead, they rode to U.S. Route 2.

Twenty minutes later, they were standing on the shore of the Midston Reservoir, beside the dam.

The place was deserted. Overhead, the clouds were piling up, denser and blacker than ever, although no rain fell yet. The gray air blinked; long seconds later, thunder grumbled. The surface of the reservoir was like a sheet of lead, with barely a ripple stirring, so that the pine trees were reflected dully in it. Inside their raincoats the three sweated in the still, oppressive heat. Not a bird sang.

"It's eerie," said Irene, speaking in a low voice as if she were unwilling to disturb the silence. "It makes you think of all those houses buried under the lake."

Danny was already scrambling down the rocky slope toward the bottom of the dam. The water rushing over the spillway on the far side ran into a stream in a ravine below and flowed away between ledges of rock, but most of the space along the foot of the dam was dry. Danny climbed among the stones, and stood looking up at the smooth, sloping wall of concrete.

It reared above him as high as a house at its highest point, grayish white and curving from shore to shore. He walked along it, still gazing upward. Irene and Joe waited, watching him.

All at once, he called, "Come on down. Quick!"

They threaded their way down among the rocks until they were standing beside him.

"What'd you find?" Joe asked.

Danny pointed to a spot some distance above his head. In the concrete, there was a crack about two feet long and wide enough to admit the blade of a knife. Brown water was oozing slowly out of it and trickling down the face.

Joe shrugged. "What does that prove?" he said. "The last time we were here, that workman said old concrete always has a few cracks."

"Yeah, I know," said Danny. "If you look higher up, and over to the right, you can see a couple. But they aren't much thicker

than a hair and there isn't any water really running out of them. This one is different— it's a real opening."

"Oh!" Irene exclaimed suddenly. "Look!"

Before their eyes, the crack had seemed to jump. It was longer, a couple of inches longer, and wider. Not much, but enough so that a real stream of water, as thick as a pencil, came bubbling out.

"Is that proof enough for you?" Danny cried. "Let's get out of here. We've got to tell somebody!"

11
The Storm Breaks

As they clambered back up to the road, a puff of wind sent ripples scudding across the surface of the reservoir. The tops of the trees bent as if a hand had passed over them. A few heavy drops fell, and a spear of lightning sizzled across the sky. It was followed by a violent crash as if the bottom had fallen out of everything. Then, down came the rain in sheets.

Danny had to shout to make himself heard. "Maybe the Professor's home—best one to tell—"

Irene nodded. The rain was beating into her face so hard that she could barely open her mouth. Joe was already getting on his bike. He had forgotten to wear a hat and his hair was plastered down on his head like a tight-fitting skullcap.

By the time they got to Danny's house, they had been so splashed by passing cars and soaked by the downpour that they could do nothing but stand dripping on the floor of the laboratory for a full minute, trying to collect their wits. Professor Bullfinch came out of his study and stared at them in surprise.

"What on earth have you been up to—riding around in this storm?" he said. "Take off your coats and hang them on those pegs before you drown in them."

"Golly!" said Joe. "I feel as if I'm soggy right through to the middle of my insides. Even my brain is soggy."

While the children hung their coats up, the professor poked around in the clutter of the laboratory and found a small electric heater. He plugged it in and said, "Stand in front of this."

"But listen!" Danny said. "There's something very important we have to tell you."

"You can tell me while you're drying off, can't you?" the Professor said reasonably.

Danny joined his friends, crouching in front of the delicious warmth. His trousers began steaming. He said, "Professor, you remember the day you were working on a container for the Irenium?"

"How could I forget it?"

"Well, we had just come from Mr. Blaze's factory with a sample of the waste that's coming out of his filter tank. We had it in a little birch-bark bucket, and when we went to help you get unstuck, I hung the bucket on the faucet of the sink."

"It's not there now," said the Professor. "I seem to recall it. But if you're going to ask me whether I took it—"

"No. Joe took it, it's his. All the liquid in it had leaked out into the sink. Go look in the sink."

Professor Bullfinch did so. With a puzzled air, he said, "The sink's empty."

"Right," said Danny. "And do you see the the crack in the concrete? Now look underneath, on the floor. Do you see the crack there, too?"

Hands on knees, the Professor squatted to look. "Yes," he said. "But I don't understand."

"Well, the filter tank at Mr. Blaze's factory is leaking, too. It must have a crack in it. That stuff—the sulfate salt—eats its way right through concrete."

"Danny!" The Professor straightened up. "You're leaping to conclusions, aren't you?"

"You've always told me that nothing is impossible," said Danny. "Some things are just a little harder to believe than others. Before the rain started we were checking the dam at the reservoir. It's concrete, too, you know. And—"

"Don't tell me you found a leak there!" said the Professor.

Quickly, Danny told what they had seen. Irene and Joe joined in. The Professor rubbed his chin, pondering, while the three friends, silent at last, watched him.

He studied both cracks again. Finally, he said, "It's certainly possible. I think I see how it could have happened. Let's leave the explanations for the time being. The first thing to do, obviously, is to warn the Water Board. Let me see, the chief engineer there is a Mr. Sawers. I've met him."

He went to his office with the three trailing behind, and picked up the phone. When a voice answered, he asked for Mr. Sawers, and said, "This is Professor Euclid Bullfinch. Yes, that's right. Now, listen carefully. I have some very disturbing information. There is a crack in the Midston dam."

He listened for a moment and said, "How do I know?" He glanced at Danny and went on. "Why—ah—it has been reported to me by a very trustworthy observer." Again, the tinny voice at the other end said something, and the Professor began to look annoyed. "Yes," he said, "I know perfectly well that dams often show slight cracks. This is nothing like that. You know who I am, and you know that I am not accustomed to talking nonsense. I'll explain everything to you later, but meanwhile this is an emergency. As far as I can tell, there's a surfactant in the water which will propagate a kind of corrosion cracking. You can understand that, can't you? Never mind how I know. What are you going to do about it?"

The other voice spoke again. Then the Professor said, "I see. That's serious. Very well. No, I don't know how much time you might have, but don't take any chances. Yes, I'll get back to you. Good-bye."

He hung up and turned to the children with a grave face.

"What did he say?" Danny asked eagerly.

"He said he would take steps to warn all the people below the dam at once," answered the Professor. "And he's sending a crew out there. They have been having some trouble with the emergency gate of the spillway, and this rain has taken them by surprise. He hopes they can get it open before anything happens."

"I remember," said Danny, "when we first went to the dam, a workman there showed us the spillway and told us about the emergency gate. It lets water out of the reservoir, doesn't it, to take the pressure off the dam."

Irene glanced out at the rain drumming down. "There's going to be a lot more water in the reservoir. Won't the pressure build up?"

"It will," said the Professor. He began to walk back and forth, frowning and fumbling in his pockets for his pipe. "If the cracks spread—"

Irene wrung her hands in distress. "There must be *something* we can do!" she said.

"I suppose," said Joe, "it wouldn't do any good to put our fingers in the dam the way that Dutch boy stuck his finger in the dike?"

Danny grabbed him by the arm. "That's it!" he cried.

"Stick our fingers in the dike?" said Joe.

"No—stick the dam together!" shouted Danny. "Professor! Won't your glue hold it? At least, until they can open the gate?"

Professor Bullfinch blinked at the boy. "I don't see why not," he said slowly. Then, with mounting enthusiasm, "By George, I think you've got something. We can certainly try it."

"But have you enough glue?" said Irene.

"Yes, I have three good-size containers," the Professor replied. "I had planned to send one to my friend, Dr. Grimes, at the American Science Foundation, and turn another over to the Midston University labs for testing. This is more important."

"Then what are we waiting for?" Danny said. "Let's go!"

The Professor put on his raincoat and jammed an old tweed hat on his head. He shoved the three containers of Irenium into the capacious pockets of his coat. Danny and his friends had struggled into their own coats, and they all stepped out into the storm.

The rain was coming down harder than ever. Now and again, thunder growled, but more distantly. They piled into the Professor's small car, which soon began to smell of wet raincoat. Its windows steamed over and everyone wiped busily with hands or handkerchiefs so that the Professor could see where he was going. The rain was so heavy that the windshield wipers could hardly keep up with it, and the Professor had to drive slowly, although Danny kept saying, "Hurry!" under his breath.

By the time they got to the dam, the rain had slackened somewhat. The Professor parked just off the road and they all but fell out of the car in their haste. There was a truck nearby, and over at the far end of the dam they could see three or four men working at the spillway. A regular waterfall was pouring over that spot which was lower than the rest of the dam, and this made their work more difficult.

Dan led the way to the edge of the slope. In the ravine at the foot of the dam, the stream had risen, fed by the spillway, and was foaming among the rocks, but it was still possible to get close to the dam itself.

Danny pointed, "I can see the water coming out of that crack," he cried. "Hurry!"

The Professor stopped. "I can't," he said helplessly. "I can't see anything." His glasses were fogged and streaming with rain.

"We'll lead you," said Danny.

He seized the Professor's hand and began to draw him toward the slope. The Professor stumbled on a stone and almost fell.

"No," he said, pulling his hand away. "It's no good, Dan. I'll break my neck. And even if I got down there, I wouldn't be able to see what I was doing."

"Give us the glue," said Joe.

Professor Bullfinch hesitated only for a moment. Then he took the three containers out of his pockets and handed them over to Danny.

"Let's go." Danny started down toward the base of the dam, sliding among the wet stones.

Joe followed him. Irene tugged at the Professor's coat sleeve.

"The workmen are yelling something at us," she said. "I'll bet they want to stop us. You'll have to talk to them, Professor."

"Don't worry. I'll explain everything to them," answered the Professor. "Go ahead."

And as Irene picked her way down to join the others, he carefully made his way to the wide walkway on the top of the dam, where one of the men who had been working on the emergency gate was waving his arms and shouting at the children.

Dan paid no attention. He reached the foot of the dam, and wiping his wet face, stared up at the concrete surface. A stream of water was spouting from the crack he had first seen. There were two other cracks now, smaller ones, but with jets of water coming from them as well. They were all too far above his head for him to reach.

"Goog! It's wet," spluttered Joe, trying to shield his eyes from the rain. "How are we going to get to them?"

"I'm the lightest," Irene said. "You two bend over and put your hands against the dam. I'll climb up on your backs. I'm sure I can reach them."

She took one of the containers from Danny, who showed her how to release the glue. Then he and Joe bent over and braced themselves.

Irene was an agile girl, but she was hampered by the beating rain, which made everything slippery, and by the container of glue. Twice she tried to get up on the boys' backs, and twice she slipped off.

Up above, the Professor and the workman were arguing. It seemed to Irene, glancing upward, that the cracks in the dam were growing larger before her eyes. She gritted her teeth and transferred the container to her left hand. Gripping Dan's shoulder with her right hand, she heaved herself up once more. This time, she managed it.

Shakily, she drew herself erect, one foot on Danny's back, the other on Joe's.

"Don't slip," Dan gasped.

She took the container in her right hand

and braced herself with her left palm against the wall of the dam. Forcing the nozzle of the can against the top of the largest crack, she pressed the lever. The glue spurted out like toothpaste from a squashed tube.

It filled the crack. And as it touched the wet concrete, it began to gleam like ice. To Irene's eager gaze, it seemed that the rain itself, as it fell upon the glue, began to thicken and solidify over the crack.

Holding the lever down, she moved the nozzle along the crack. Slowly, the stream of water coming from it dwindled, became a trickle, and then stopped altogether.

"It works!" she screeched.

That container was empty. Cautiously, she reached down, tapped Dan on the shoulder, and got another from him. Rapidly, she pressed the nozzle against the other two cracks and sealed them with glue, too. She tossed away the empty container and, putting her head back, shouted as loudly as she could: "Professor! Can you hear me?"

Professor Bullfinch bent over, peering down, trying to make her out through the wet lenses of his glasses. "I hear you. What is it?"

"The leaks have stopped!"

"Good. Get away from there, then, quick!"

She started to get down. Her foot slid on Dan's wet raincoat and she fell, bringing both boys down with her. They untangled themselves and got to their feet.

"You're going to have to go on a diet," Joe groaned, rubbing his back.

From above, the workman yelled, "Get out of there, you kids! They're going to open the gate."

The three began climbing to the road as fast as they could. They reached it, turned, and looked back. The men had freed the emergency gate. A great rush of water went pouring over the spillway, filling the ravine below and rising halfway up the slope.

The Professor and the workman who had been talking to him joined the children at the end of the dam.

"That's taken some of the pressure off," said the workman. "But what about this stuff of yours—how long will it hold?"

"I don't know," said the Professor.

"Well, it's given us a little more time to warn everybody," said the workman. "Now we'd better all get going. If the dam breaks, this whole road and everything around it is going to be underwater."

He started to move away, and stopped. "You people may be crazy," he said, "but if that stuff really works, you ought to get the biggest medals the town can give you."

12
"An Unexpected Effect . . ."

The storm had blown itself away, grumbling and snarling to the east, and by evening the clouds had broken into a glorious sunset. All that afternoon and into the night, men from the Water Board had watched the dam for any further signs of cracking, while they waited for the weather to clear so that they could get to work on reinforcing it. Early next morning, they had inspected the concrete and had found three other small leaks. After Mr. Sawers, the engineer, had had a conference with Professor Bullfinch, he had used some of the new glue to plug them with. At the same time, he had begun the preparations for emergency repairs.

"And the Irenium is still holding," the Professor announced with satisfaction.

He had just returned from the dam. The living room of the house was rather crowded, for in addition to Mrs. Dunn and some of the members of her committee, the mayor, Mr. Narciso, was there, as well as Mr. Popple, the director of the Water Board, a reporter from the *Midston Chronicle,* and a photographer who lurked in corners and snapped pictures. And, of course, Danny, Irene, and Joe.

"Luckily," the Professor continued, "the cracking is confined to that small area, so far. Mr. Sawers thinks there may have been a weak place there. But after all, the dam is forty-five years old."

"I still don't understand what happened," said Mr. Narciso. "You say it was that waste from the Blaze factory. But the stuff was harmless! We saw Mr. Starling drink it at the hearing."

"It is perfectly harmless—to people," said the Professor. "What happened was, frankly, an unexpected effect. You see, this sulfate salt is what we call a surfactant. It has an affinity for the surfaces of things—it coats them, and clings to them. It is something like a detergent. A detergent—the stuff you wash dishes in—moves through the dishwasher and coats the surface of dishes and the surfaces of grease particles. It keeps them from sticking together, and that's how the dishes are washed free of grease.

"This organic sulfate salt is a member of that same family. It has a special affinity for some alumina compounds in concrete. When it is able to work its way into a crack, it clings to the surfaces as if it were a detergent and wedges them farther and farther apart so that they cannot rejoin. By degrees, the crack grows larger and begins to spread until the whole surface is affected."

"It seems clear," said Mr. Popple, of the Water Board, "that what happened was that the stuff cracked the filter tank at the factory in just that way. It oozed out, saturated the ground, and found its way down into the water table. It made its way into the stream and into the reservoir, just as Mrs. Dunn's committee said. The stream flows into the reservoir near the dam, and over the past year a concentration of the sulfate salt has been building up at that point, moved there by the current."

Mr. Narciso turned to Mrs. Dunn. "You people were right, then," he said. "It's all tied together."

"Yes," said Mrs. Dunn firmly. "What we're concerned about is what the Professor has called 'unexpected effects.' Because everything is tied together—the water, the air, the land —we have to go slowly and try to study the effects of what we do *before* we do it. I know it sometimes looks as though we're holding back progress, or keeping people from having jobs. But sometimes, *afterward* can be too late. Just think what would have happened in this case if Danny and Irene and Joe hadn't had the sense to follow up the clues they found, from the very beginning!"

She glanced at Danny, who was grinning sheepishly, his face crimson. "My son did a lot of things that were wrong," she said. "But I'm proud of him. And of the other children, too."

She was interrupted by a loud knocking at the front door. "Who on earth—?" she said. "Excuse me."

She went into the hall to open the door. Everyone in the living room heard her exclaim, "Oh! It's you!"

A moment later, she returned. With her was Mr. Blaze.

He came in with his big head thrust forward, as usual, and his heavy eyebrows drawn together in a scowl. He stood with his stumpy legs apart, his hands behind his back. Everyone stared at him in astonishment.

"I've been told what's happened," he said.

Mr. Narciso cleared his throat nervously. "Now, Mr. Blaze," he said, "I hope you aren't here to make trouble."

"Trouble? Certainly not," bellowed Mr. Blaze. "I'm here to see that boy—where is he?"

"Does he mean me?" said Joe, in an undertone. "If he does, I'm not here."

"You mean me?" Danny said.

"That's right," said Mr. Blaze. "Here. Take this."

He thrust out his hand. There was an envelope in it. Danny came forward and took it uncertainly. He opened it.

"Read it," said Mr. Blaze. "Out loud."

Slowly, Dan took out a folded piece of paper. He read: " 'Your mother was right and I was wrong. I apologize. Yours, J. R. Blaze.' "

There was something else in the envelope: two five-dollar bills and a one-dollar bill.

"That's your money," Mr. Blaze said in a voice that had suddenly grown mild. "I guess a pair of pants was worth the lesson."

Danny was too flabbergasted to thank him. He could only stand, holding the eleven dollars and the note, with his mouth open.

All the grownups began talking at once. Danny turned away, glanced at his friends, and jerked his head toward the door. A moment or two later all three children had slipped into the hall. No one saw them go.

"What's up?" Joe said softly.

"Nothing. I just wanted to get out of there," said Danny. "I had a feeling they were all going to start thanking us again."

"There's nothing wrong with that," Joe said. "I kind of enjoyed those nice things your mother said. In fact, I wrote a poem about it."

"All right," said Irene. "Let's go outside where we can listen in peace."

They opened the front door and went out into the hot, bright day. Joe took a piece of paper out of his shirt pocket, cleared his throat, and read:

> Professor Bullfinch invented a marvelous glue,
> That's true.
> But he did it because of some help, you must agree,
> From we.

Irene squealed with laughter. "That's not good English, Joe."

"Okay. I'll change it," Joe said.

> He did it, you must admit, because of
> the stimulus
> From us.

"Great," Danny said, shaking his head. Joe went on:

> Although he owes all his success to the
> brilliance with which we are endowed,
> We are not proud.
> We do not ask for medals or monuments
> or temples or pagodas.
> All we want are ice-cream sodas.

Dan and Irene applauded. "Golly," Irene said, "he does that the way we do math problems."

"He's a wonder," Danny agreed. "Come on, then."

"Come on where?" asked Joe suspiciously. "Not another of your crazy projects?"

"No, no," said Danny. "I've got this eleven dollars, and I have to go to the bank with it, and I thought that on the way we could stop and spend some of it just as Joe suggests. We deserve it."

He linked his arms with the other two. They went off down the street, singing at the tops of their voices,

We do not asks for medals or pagodas—
Just ice-cream sodas!

ABOUT THE AUTHORS
AND ILLUSTRATOR

JAY WILLIAMS has written over twenty-five fiction and nonfiction books for children of all ages, in addition to coauthoring fifteen books about Danny Dunn. Mr. Williams was born in Buffalo, New York, and educated at the University of Pennsylvania, Columbia University, and the Art Students League.

RAYMOND ABRASHKIN wrote and co-produced the very popular and successful "Little Fugitive," a film that won an award at the Venice Film Festival.

PAUL SAGSOORIAN was born in New York City and studied art at several art schools there. A free-lance illustrator, he works for art studios, advertising agencies, and book publishers.

There's No Stopping

Danny Dunn!

Danny Dunn, science fiction hero, with his friends,
Irene and Joe, can't stay away from mystery and
adventure. They have shrunk to the size of insects,
traveled back in time, sunk to the ocean floor,
and rocketed through outer space!

**The DANNY DUNN books,
by Jay Williams and Raymond Abrashkin:**

ARCHWAY PAPERBACKS from Pocket Books